Teggs is no ord
he's an **ASTRO**
the amazing spaces
goes on dangerous missions and fights
evil – along with his faithful crew,
Gipsy, Arx and Iggy!

*Read all the adventures of
Teggs, Gipsy, Arx and Iggy!*

RIDDLE OF THE RAPTORS
THE HATCHING HORROR
THE SEAS OF DOOM
THE MIND-SWAP MENACE
THE SKIES OF FEAR
THE SPACE GHOSTS
DAY OF THE DINO-DROIDS
THE TERROR-BIRD TRAP
Coming soon
THE PLANET OF PERIL

Free collector cards in all these Astrosaurs books!
More cards available from
www.astrosaurs.co.uk

For Jill
I would never have got here without you

TEETH OF THE T. REX
A RED FOX BOOK 978 1 862 30285 3

First published in Great Britain by Red Fox,
an imprint of Random House Children's Books
This edition published 2007

1 3 5 7 9 10 8 6 4 2

Papers used by Random House Children's Books are natural, recyclable
products made from wood grown in sustainable forests. The manufacturing
processes conform to the environmental regulations of the country of origin.

Typeset in Bembo Schoolbook by Palimpsest Book Production Ltd,
Grangemouth, Stirlingshire

Red Fox Books are published by Random House Children's Books,
61–63 Uxbridge Road, London W5 5SA,
a division of The Random House Group Ltd,
in Australia by Random House Australia (Pty) Ltd,
20 Alfred Street, Milsons Point, Sydney, NSW 2061, Australia,
in New Zealand by Random House New Zealand Ltd,
18 Poland Road, Glenfield, Auckland 10, New Zealand,
in South Africa by Random House (Pty) Ltd,
Isle of Houghton, Corner of Boundary Road & Carse O'Gowrie,
Houghton 2198, South Africa,
and in India by Random House India Pvt Ltd,
301 World Trade Tower, Hotel Intercontinental Grand Complex,
Barakhamba Lane, New Delhi 110 001, India

THE RANDOM HOUSE GROUP Limited Reg. No. 954009
www.kidsatrandomhouse.co.uk

A CIP catalogue record for this book is available from the British Library.

Printed and bound in Great Britain by
Bookmarque Limited, Croydon, Surrey

Astrosaurs

TEETH OF THE T. REX

Steve Cole

Illustrated by Woody Fox

RED FOX

WARNING!

THINK YOU KNOW ABOUT DINOSAURS?

THINK AGAIN!

The dinosaurs . . .

Big, stupid, lumbering reptiles. Right?

All they did was eat, sleep and roar a bit. Right?

Died out millions of years ago when a big meteor struck the Earth. Right?

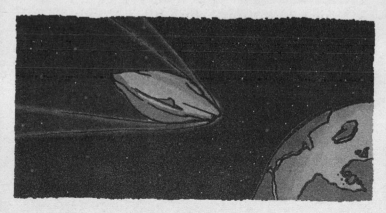

Wrong!

The dinosaurs weren't stupid. They may have had small brains, but they used them well. They had big thoughts and big dreams.

By the time the meteor hit, the last dinosaurs had already left Earth for ever. Some breeds had discovered how to travel through space as early as the Triassic period, and were already enjoying a new life among the stars. No one has found evidence of dinosaur technology yet. But the first fossil bones were only unearthed in 1822, and new finds are being made all the time.

The proof is out there, buried in the ground.

And the dinosaurs live on, way out in space, even now. They've settled down in a place they call the Jurassic Quadrant and over the last sixty-five million years they've gone on evolving.

The dinosaurs we'll be meeting are part of a special group called the Dinosaur Space Service. Their job is to explore space, to go on exciting missions and to fight evil and protect the innocent!

These heroic herbivores are not just dinosaurs.

They are *astrosaurs*!

NOTE: The following story has been translated from secret Dinosaur Space Service records. Earthling dinosaur names are used throughout, although some changes have been made for easy reading.

TALKING DINOSAUR!

How to say the dinosaur
names in this book . . .

STEGOSAURUS –
STEG-oh-SORE-us

TRICERATOPS –
try-SERRA-tops

IGUANODON –
ig-WA-noh-don

HADROSAUR –
HAD-roh-sore

DIMORPHODON –
die-MORF-oh-don

THE CREW OF THE
DSS SAUROPOD

**CAPTAIN
TEGGS STEGOSAUR**

ARX ORANO,
FIRST OFFICER

GIPSY SAURINE,
COMMUNICATIONS
OFFICER

IGGY TOOTH,
CHIEF ENGINEER

Jurassic Quadrant

Ankylos

Steggos

Diplox

INDEPENDEN
DINOSAUR
ALLIANCE

vegetarian
sector

Squawk
Major

DSS
UNION OF
PLANETS

PTEROSAURIA

Tri System

Corytho

Lambeos

Iguanos

Aqua Minor

Geldos Cluster

Teerex
Major

Olympus

TYRANNOSAUR
TERRITORIES

carnivore
sector

Raptos

Planet Sixty

THEROPOD EMPIRE

Cryptos

Megalos

vegmeat
zone
(neutral space)

SEA REPTILE
SPACE

Pliosaur
Nurseries

Not to scale

Chapter One

DINOS IN DISTRESS

The spaceship zoomed past stars and planets on its latest exciting mission.

It was a ship full of dinosaurs! They were all different sizes and all different types. On the flight deck alone there were a stegosaurus, a triceratops, an iguanodon and a stripy hadrosaur, not to mention a flock of dimorphodon

1

– fifty flying reptiles that worked the ship's switches and levers with their beaks and claws.

The stegosaurus sat chomping on a big clump of grass. His name was Captain Teggs, and the spaceship was called the DSS *Sauropod*. It was the finest ship in the Dinosaur Space Service – with the best-stocked kitchen in the universe. Teggs's favourite things in life were scoffing food and having adventures, and he was always on the look-out for ways to combine the two.

Teggs turned in his control pit to the green triceratops beside him. "Anything to report, Arx?"

"All quiet, Captain," said Arx, Teggs's dinosaur deputy.

Right now they were on border patrol in the no-man's land between the Vegetarian Sector – where all the plant-eaters lived – and the Carnivore Sector, where no plant-eater would dare set foot! The sneaky meat-eaters often launched surprise attacks, and ships like the *Sauropod* had to stop them.

"Wait!" cried the stripy hadrosaur, putting a hoof to her headphones. Her name was Gipsy and she was in charge of the ship's communications. "I'm picking up a mysterious message. I think it's a distress signal!" Then she gasped and pulled the headphones away. "Ow! It's very loud. Ships for millions of miles around will pick up that message."

Teggs rose up from the control pit. He was as big as a truck, with jagged bony plates running down his orange-brown back. "Quick," he said, "let's hear it through the main speakers."

Gipsy put the signal through – but the second she did, the speakers EXPLODED! The dimorphodon flapped around in fright.

"That's what I call *loud*!" cried Iggy, the iguanodon engineer. "Shall I fix the speakers, Captain? Won't take me a sec."

Teggs nodded. He knew Iggy was brilliant with anything mechanical.

With a last rattle of wires, Iggy finished his repairs. "All done!"

"Play the message again, Gipsy," Teggs said. "Only this time, turn down the volume!"

A gruff female voice burst from the speakers. Even on lowest volume, it shook the flight deck.

"*Um . . . help. Ooooh dear. We is needing, er, helpful dinosaurs to . . . um . . . help us. Come here NOW! Er, please.*"

"That's the message, Captain," said Gipsy. "I've sent a greeting signal but there's no reply."

Teggs frowned. "Whoever they are, it doesn't sound like they're used to asking for help."

"But they're very keen that *someone* hears that message," said Iggy. "That's why the volume's so high."

Arx checked his space radar. "There is a small ship drifting close by. The message must be coming from there."

"Let's see it on the scanner," said Teggs.

A dimorphodon flapped down and pecked the scanner control with his beak. A crumpled grey ship with no markings appeared on the screen, floating beside a large asteroid.

"I've never seen a ship like that before," said Iggy. "Looks like it's been in a crash."

"Still no reply to my signal," said Gipsy.

Teggs rushed to the lift. "Come on, Gipsy, let's check out that ship. Arx, Iggy – stay on full alert till we get back."

The astrosaurs saluted. "Yes, Captain!"

Teggs and Gipsy put on their space armour, just in case of trouble. Then they jumped in a shuttle – one of the six short-range spaceships the *Sauropod* carried – and flew over to the battered ship.

They got inside through a loading bay. The ship's corridors were long and shadowy, and smelled of stale pies and old socks. Gipsy wished she could put a peg on her snout.

"Anyone at home?" Teggs called.

There was no reply.

"Let's go to the control room," Teggs

7

suggested. "Perhaps we'll find the crew there."

They soon found the control room. The crew weren't there – but something else *was*. A big, bumpy bundle wrapped up in red fur sat on a table in the middle of the room.

"What do you suppose *that* is?" whispered Gipsy.

"Only one way to find out," said Teggs.

He stretched out the tip of his spiky tail and whipped away the red fur. Lying underneath were a wonky golden crown, a gleaming staff shaped like a long claw, a heavy metal chain – and a big bronze skull!

"Yuk!" said Gipsy. "Those things are horrible." Then she noticed a red light flashing on a control panel and went to see. "Captain!" she gasped. "This *machine* sent the distress call. No wonder no one replied to me – it's just a recording!"

But Teggs barely heard her. He had picked up the crown – and found writing scratched into the back. It read:

Thiss krown bellongs to t. rex King
Anywun else touching it will DIE

"Gipsy, these are the T. rex Crown Jewels!" Teggs whispered. "I remember

9

hearing they were stolen from the king's palace last year. He's been searching for them ever since . . ."

Suddenly his communicator bleeped. It was Arx. "Captain, quick!" the triceratops shouted. "A big ship has come out from behind that asteroid and is heading your way. It looks like a carnivore craft – get out of there, fast!"

Teggs gulped. "Come on, Gipsy, back to the shuttle!"

"STAY STILL!" came a deafening roar behind them. "OR US EAT YOU!"

Teggs twirled round to find that four huge scaly nightmares in blood-red uniforms had squeezed inside the control room. Each one was as big as a bungalow with legs as thick as tree-trunks. They had claws like razors and piggy little eyes. Their drooling jaws bristled with knife-sharp teeth the size of bananas.

"Oh, *no!*" Gipsy gulped. "T. rexes!"

Teggs nodded grimly. "We're in trouble now!"

The leader of the monsters stomped towards them. "Us Royal Rex Police," it growled. "You been caught red-handed with our Crown Jewels. Surrender – or DIE!"

Chapter Two

TRIAL BY T. REX

"You are making a mistake," Teggs
warned the colossal carnivore, whirling
his armoured tail above his head.

But the T. rex leader lunged at him!

Gipsy jabbed it in the leg with her
snout, and Teggs whacked it on the
end of its nose. It staggered back and
knocked over another T. rex. But a
third was already pounding over to get
them. Gipsy dived forward and skidded
underneath its legs, delivering ten judo
chops in a single second as she went.
With its legs knocked from under it,
the T. rex couldn't fight back as Teggs

reared up and pushed it over.

But then another of the giant carnivores grabbed Gipsy with its nasty, pinchy claws. "Surrender!" it roared at Teggs. "Or us EAT her."

The bony plates along Teggs's back flushed red with anger. "Watch it, meat-chops!" he snarled. "We are astrosaurs on a mission, answering a distress call. Under Jurassic law sub-section one-point-three paragraph nine – you *can't* eat us."

"Really?" The T. rex looked disappointed. "Oh."

"Lucky you know so much about the law, Captain," hissed Gipsy.

"I don't!" Teggs hissed back. "I just made that up!"

"Us not eat you anyway," sneered the T. rex leader, getting back up and producing two sets of handcuffs. "Us do

14

things proper. You under arrest for stealing."

"But we didn't steal anything!" cried Gipsy as she was roughly cuffed.

The leader ignored her and cuffed Teggs too. "Us take you to our planet, put you on trial and send you to prison," he grunted. "THEN we eat you!"

All the T. rexes roared with nasty laughter as Teggs and Gipsy were dragged struggling away . . .

An hour later, Iggy and the dimorphodon watched helplessly as the police ship took off for the Carnivore Sector with Teggs and Gipsy aboard. The T. rex leader had appeared on the scanner to tell them what had happened – and to warn the *Sauropod* not to follow them.

"This isn't fair!" cried Iggy.

Just then, Arx came back to the flight deck. He looked weary and cross.

"I tried to tell Admiral Rosso about Teggs and Gipsy," said Arx. Rosso was the crusty old barosaurus in charge of the Dinosaur Space Service. "It was no good. He's away on a space expedition and won't be back till late tomorrow."

"But we've got to do something!" Iggy exclaimed.

"I also talked to the T. rex ambassador," Arx went on. "I explained that Teggs and Gipsy were tricked into going aboard that ship by a fake distress call. I said that the Crown Jewels must have been placed there for them to find. I pointed out what a coincidence it was that there just happened to be a Royal Rex Police ship close by. And I urged him to set Teggs and Gipsy free so we can help find the *real* villains."

Iggy nodded eagerly. "What did he say?"

"He burped, made a rude noise with his bottom and fell asleep!" Arx sighed. "You just can't reason with a T. rex."

"So what happens to Teggs and Gipsy now?" asked Iggy.

Arx looked worried. "They will be sent to Claw Court on the planet Teerex Major."

"Good," said Iggy. "The judge will soon see they are innocent."

"I'm not so sure," said Arx. "This trial will be led by Judge Braxus the Bloodthirsty – the toughest, meanest judge in the entire Jurassic Quadrant!"

Teggs and Gipsy huddled together in the middle of the T. rex Claw Court. It was a large, dark building that stank of rotten meat and armpits. Bones and bloodstains covered the floor. Sitting all around were jeering, drooling T. rexes who had come to watch the trial. Each was as tall as three elephants, and the astrosaurs felt very small in comparison.

"I wish they had let us keep our armour," said Teggs. "I feel naked without it!"

"I wish Arx was allowed to defend us," Gipsy said sadly.

"He'd get us off just like that!" Teggs agreed. "Unlike our useless lump of a lawyer there."

A T. rex in a little grey wig was sitting to one side. She was supposed to be sticking up for them today — but since she had already tried to eat them twice in the last half-hour, Teggs wasn't sure her heart was really in it.

"All stand!" someone growled. "Here come Judge Braxus!"

The watching crowd jumped up, roaring and cheering, as a squat, ugly T. rex in red robes and a bloodstained wig swaggered inside and perched on a tall chair. "Silence in court!" he shouted. "Or me kill you!"

The courtroom fell silent.

"Hey, you! Astrosaur scumballs!" said Braxus. "How does you bleed?"

"You mean, 'How do you *plead*?'," Teggs corrected him.

Braxus grinned nastily. "Me know what me means."

Gipsy turned to their lawyer. "Are you going to let him threaten us like that?"

But their lawyer was snoring. She had fallen asleep!

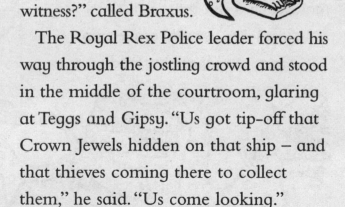

"Where is first witness?" called Braxus.

The Royal Rex Police leader forced his way through the jostling crowd and stood in the middle of the courtroom, glaring at Teggs and Gipsy. "Us got tip-off that Crown Jewels hidden on that ship – and that thieves coming there to collect them," he said. "Us come looking."

"But we were tricked into going

21

there," said Teggs. "We were answering a distress call that turned out to be a rotten recording! Whoever tipped you off must have left the Crown Jewels on that ship and used a fake distress call to lure us on board – knowing that you would find us!"

"Rubbish," shouted Judge Braxus. "Me find you GUILTY!"

"That's not fair!" cried Gipsy.

But the crowd went wild. "*Guilty! Guilty!*" they chanted in delight. They made such a din that even the astrosaurs' lawyer was woken up.

"Objection!" she spluttered.

"Me EAT anyone who objects," Braxus warned her.

The lawyer turned to Teggs and Gipsy. "Bye," she grunted – and ran for it!

"Me find astrosaur scumballs VERY guilty," Braxus went on. "You be sent to Saint Bonecracker's Prison – worst prison on Teerex Major."

"You can't do this to us!" Teggs shouted.

"Can so too!" Braxus retorted. "Me send you there for ten years – but you probably be eaten in ten MINUTES. Ha, ha, ha!"

The judge's laughter mingled with the howls and shrieks of the T. rex hordes all around them. Gipsy and Teggs hugged each other as the racket rocked Claw

Court to its foundations. "We've been in some tight scrapes before, Gipsy," said Teggs grimly. "But never as tight as *this!*"

Chapter Three

PRISONERS!

Teggs and Gipsy were booted out of
Claw Court and chucked into a T. rex
police shuttle. It took them straight to St
Bonecracker's prison, an enormous
towering castle that looked as dark and
scary as a hundred haunted houses
rolled into one.

Inside it was no better. The smell of sweaty claws and dirty bottoms filled the air. The warders were huge, clanking robots that fired laser beams from their eyes if anyone misbehaved. Teggs and Gipsy had to take off their astrosaur uniforms and wear nasty grey prison outfits, stained with things Teggs didn't like to think about.

Then the robots took the new arrivals to report to the prison governor – Mrs Fangetta.

"Welcome to my prison, plant-eating scum!" growled Fangetta. She was warty and extremely ugly. Around her waist she wore a shabby tutu that was the same sickly pink colour as her eyes.

"Me not think you like it here much!"

Gipsy gave her a hard stare. "When the Dinosaur Space Service hears about this, you're going to be in big trouble."

"Unless you let us go now," Teggs added hopefully.

Fangetta started laughing. "Let you go? That a good one." She tried to hold her ribs, but her feeble arms weren't quite long enough. "Ha ha ha, my sides is splitting!"

Suddenly Teggs noticed a framed photo on Fangetta's desk. It was a picture of her cuddling Braxus the Bloodthirsty!

"I see you know our judge," he remarked.

At once, Fangetta stopped laughing. Her pink eyes narrowed. "Braxus send many crooks here. Him decent, upstanding T. rex."

Gipsy stared at her. "But he's a bonkers, bloodthirsty maniac!"

"To a T. rex, that *is* decent and upstanding," Teggs reminded her.

"Me not have you talk about my lickle Braxie-waxie like this," she roared, thwumping her tail against the floor so hard that the door of the cupboard behind her fell open – to reveal something surprising.

"Hang on," said Gipsy. "Aren't those the Crown Jewels we're supposed to have stolen?"

"Yes!" Teggs frowned. "How come *you've* got them?"

Fangetta looked suddenly shifty. "Um . . . This be prison. Good place to lock things up safe. Me guarding the jewels till King Groosum get here."

"The T. rex ruler is coming *here*?" said Gipsy, the crest on her head flushing blue with alarm.

"Yeah!" Fangetta gave her a nasty smile. "Him want to meet you. Him want to teach you lesson you never forget. Then us hold special feast in his honour, and give him back Crown Jewels."

"Sounds fun," joked Teggs. "What a shame we won't be able to go."

"Maybe you will," said Fangetta

mysteriously. "Warders, take them to their cells — before me eats them NOW!"

Gipsy and Teggs looked at each other helplessly as the robots clanked back into the room and yanked them away . . .

Back on the *Sauropod*, Arx and Iggy were waiting tensely for Admiral Rosso to get back from his space expedition.

"I just don't get it," said Iggy. "Why did whoever stole the Crown Jewels suddenly want to get rid of them?"

"Maybe the jewels were just too risky to keep," said Arx. "With thousands of angry T. rex police tearing space apart for them, wouldn't *you* hand them over?"

"But why not just dump them on that ship?" Iggy wondered. "Why bother to frame someone else for the crime?"

"I don't know," said Arx. "But I know of one T. rex in particular who'll be pleased – Thickhead McBrick!"

Iggy frowned. "Who?"

"He was accused of stealing the Crown Jewels," Arx explained. "He never admitted it, but they chucked him in prison anyway. Now I suppose they'll have to let him go." He paused. "Funnily enough, he was sent to Saint Bonecracker's Prison by Braxus the Bloodthirsty too – just like Teggs and Gipsy."

"I hate to think of them in that terrible place!" cried Iggy. "Arx, we

31

can't wait any longer for Admiral
Rosso. We have to get them out of
prison!"

"We can't take a DSS ship into the
Carnivore Sector when the T. rexes
warned us not to. It could start an
intergalactic war!" said Arx. Then he
smiled. "However – if the two of us
went in a small, unmarked ship . . ."

"Of course!" Iggy cheered. "The
battered old ship that started all this is
just outside! We can travel in that!"

"Come on, then," said Arx, charging
to the lift. "If we're going to save our
friends, there's no time to lose!"

It was lunchtime back in St
Bonecrackers, and Teggs and Gipsy
were sitting in a quiet corner of the
prison canteen. They stared miserably
at their untouched bowls of maggot-

and-tailbone stew.

"I'm starving!" Teggs groaned. "You'd think this restaurant would have a vegetarian option!"

"Not when everyone else is a meat-eater," said Gipsy. She looked up from her bowl and gulped. "Uh-oh. Looks like one or two of our fellow inmates think *we* look tastier than this sloppy stew . . ."

Teggs turned and gasped. "One or two *hundred*, you mean!"

While the robot warders looked the other way, drooling T. rexes had sneaked up and surrounded them! Claws twitched and jaws snapped open and shut as the gigantic carnivores closed in on the astrosaurs . . .

Chapter Four

TUNNEL OF FEAR

"I'll hold them off," said Teggs bravely as the T. rexes lumbered closer. "Gipsy, get ready to run."

But Gipsy shook her head. "No way! If this is the end, we will face it together!"

But then help came from an unexpected source – Teggs's stomach!

RROOAAARRR! Teggs was so hungry that his tummy rumbled and growled like there were fifty ravenous raptors trapped inside! The extraordinary noise echoed around the canteen.

"Excuse me," said Teggs, rubbing his empty belly. But the T. rexes had stopped. They were watching him with fear in their eyes.

"Me never hear roar as scary as that before!" one said.

"Quick, Captain, do it again!" Gipsy urged him.

"I can't just make my tummy rumble!" he hissed back at her.

"You can! Think of a big bowl of fern falafels and carrot custard and juicy leaf risotto . . ."

Teggs did – and this time his stomach rumbled like an earthquake kicking off. *RRRRROOOOAAAAARRRRR!*

The T. rexes backed away in alarm. "Us not eating big growly thing like that!" they shouted, smashing into tables and squashing their chairs as they rushed to get away.

The robot warders finally looked up at all the ruckus going on, and started blasting at the crowd with their eye lasers. "STAND STILL OR DIE!"

Even the stupidest T. rexes understood that order, and did as they were told.

Two robot warders clanked over to the astrosaurs and grabbed them by the tails. "YOU ARE TROUBLEMAKERS," it droned. "WE WILL TAKE YOU TO MRS FANGETTA FOR PUNISHMENT."

"Can't wait." Teggs sighed.

The robots dragged them off to Fangetta's office. Someone was just coming out – a stooped, skinny T. rex who was nasty looking even by carnivore standards.

37

"Goodbye, Thickhead McBrick!" called Fangetta. "Congratulations on your release!"

"Ha!" Thickhead sniggered. "And me owe it all to you astrosaurs!"

"What are you on about?" asked Gipsy.

"Me was put in here 'cause they thought me stole Crown Jewels," said Thickhead. "Now King knows *you* did it, me has been given royal pardon. Me free!" He danced off down the corridor. "So long, suckers!"

Teggs scowled. "You know, what *really* bugs me about all this is that the real Crown Jewel thief is still at large."

"Don't talk stupid," hissed Fangetta, stomping out of her office in her grimy tutu. "Everyone knows YOU done it. Now, what you doing back here already?"

"PRISONERS CAUSED TROUBLE IN CANTEEN," said one of the warders.

"Oh dear, dear," said Fangetta, with a nasty smile. "This means PUNISH-MENT. Me send you to kitchens."

Teggs groaned. "You mean we have to help make your repulsive meaty meals?"

"Me not send you to work." Fangetta smiled. "Me send you to STEWPOT!

Your punishment is to be king's dinner at royal feast tonight. Mmm, astrosaur stew — delicious!" She licked her leathery lips, splashing drool over the floor. "Take them away!"

"You monsters!" cried Gipsy, struggling furiously against the metal grip of the warders as she and Teggs were dragged off to the kitchens . . .

Meanwhile, Arx and Iggy had reached Teerex Major in the unmarked spaceship. Arx checked his guide book. "It says that Saint Bonecracker's is in the smelliest, noisiest, dirtiest district on the planet," he reported. "I expect T. rexes are queuing up to live around there!"

They landed in a parking bay close to the prison. Iggy had brought some power tools with him. "The easiest way to get Teggs and Gipsy out of jail is to dig a tunnel," he explained. "We must dig one right under the prison walls, find them and escape back here."

"I've got a plan of the prison," said Arx, waving a piece of paper. "That should make sure we don't come out in the middle of a T. rex cell!"

They peeped out of the spaceship. The air smelled of rotten meat and old dung. Rocket-cars and space trains made a terrible racket all around. T. rex traffic wardens patrolled the bay, handing out tickets – and eating anyone who complained!

41

Arx and Iggy sneaked out when the wardens weren't looking and hid underneath the little ship. Then they started to dig their tunnel. Iggy had a super-spade and Arx used a power-pickaxe. No one could hear them working over the din of the traffic, and soon they were making good progress through the dark slimy mud.

"Let's aim for the prison library," suggested Arx, checking the map. "That should be nice and quiet – none of the T. rexes can actually read!"

"And it's not too far from the cell blocks either," Iggy noted. "Come on!"

But suddenly the roof of the tunnel began to tremble above them.

"Look out!" cried Arx. "The mud must be crumblier here. This whole section of the tunnel is going to cave in on top of us!"

"No time to go back," Iggy shouted as heavy soil started raining down about them. "We'll just have to keep going forward!"

The stocky iguanodon swung the super-spade with all his strength, faster and faster as the tunnel roof crashed down behind him. He made his tunnel slope upwards so less mud could fall in on them, digging and digging until he'd lost all track of time. Finally, once he was certain the roof above was secure, Iggy collapsed in a sweaty heap.

"Phew," he said. "That was a close one, wasn't it, Arx?"

No reply.

"Arx?" he repeated.

But Arx wasn't there!

"Oh no," groaned Iggy. "We've been cut off by the cave-in!" He yelled down the tunnel. "Arx? You'd better not be squashed flat under all that mud! Where are you?"

"WHO THAT DOWN THERE?" came a scary shout from just beyond the tunnel roof.

"Uh-oh," said Iggy, with a sinking feeling. "I don't know where I am – but I must have dug myself back up to ground level!"

Suddenly, huge scaly feet came smashing through the tunnel roof, and nasty claws reached down to yank him out of the ground. Blinking in the bright light, too exhausted from digging to run, Iggy found himself surrounded by ugly meat-eaters in scruffy dinner suits. Clunky robots were offering drinks and raw meat to the guests – and one of those robots was holding him by the tail in an unbreakable grip.

"Um . . . great party!" Iggy smiled weakly at the snarling faces all around.

"I always like to make a big entrance . . ."

Then an ugly female T. rex in a pink tutu and tiara pushed through the crowd. She was holding hands with a squat, ugly male in red robes and a bloodstained wig. "Look, Braxus!" she cried, an evil smile spreading over her face. "Us found uninvited iguanodon. Look like *another* astrosaur!"

"Him must be here to save his criminal friends, Fangetta," said Braxus. "Instead, him will join them – ON OUR DINNER PLATES!"

Chapter Five

ASTROSAUR STEW!

Teggs and Gipsy had been tied up with rope and squashed together in a big

cauldron. It stood in the corner of the prison's grandest dining room – a damp, rotten place filled with rickety tables and chairs. Beneath the cauldron was a big pile of firewood, ready to be lit.

"I wish the T. rex chef had added more potatoes to this salty water," said Teggs as he gulped the last one down. Eating helped to take his mind off the grisly fate that awaited them. "Some swampgrass would be nice too – to really bring out our full flavour."

Gipsy forced a brave smile. She knew Teggs was only joking to keep her spirits up. "Oh, Captain, I can't believe we're going to end up in a T. rex's tum!" she cried. "If only we could get out of here—"

Suddenly the dining-room door burst open.

"Iggy!" cried Gipsy, who couldn't believe her eyes.

Teggs cheered. "He's come to save us!"

"Er . . . sorry, guys," said Iggy. And

now Gipsy could see Fangetta and Braxus standing right behind him. "I got caught."

"Soon us light fire beneath you," growled Fangetta. "Then you be HOT DINNER!" She and Braxus tied Iggy up tight and plopped him into the pot.

"Thanks for trying to save us, Ig," said Gipsy fondly. "But where's Arx?"

"I don't know," Iggy admitted. "The tunnel we were digging fell in on us. We got split up." He sniffed. "I don't even know if he's still alive!"

Gipsy gasped with horror, and Teggs bowed his head. Things had never seemed more desperate. He glared at their carefree carnivore captors as they fussed over who would sit where at the royal feast.

"This where King Groosum gonna be," said Fangetta, pointing to a grotty throne. "You go on one side, me go on other side. Thickhead McBrick sit on next table."

"Thickhead?" Teggs frowned. "What's he doing here?"

"Maybe the king wants to say sorry for locking him up," said Gipsy. "After all, he thinks *we* are the real crooks now."

"When do us give King the Crown Jewels?" asked Braxus, pointing to the large red fur bundle in front of the throne.

"As soon as him come in," said Fangetta. Then she sniggered. "Us not want him to think us want to hang on to Crown Jewels . . ."

"No, us would not want him thinking that," Braxus agreed, joining in the laughter.

"What's so funny?" wondered Iggy. "Are they up to something?"

"I don't know," Gipsy admitted. "What do you think, Captain?"

"I think," Teggs spluttered as he pulled his head out from the salty water, "that the spaghetti they put in this stew is really, really tough!" Even so, he took a deep breath and ducked his head back under to go on chewing.

Suddenly a robot warder crashed into the dining room. "GUESTS ARE READY TO ENTER," it droned.

"COME IN, THEN!" Fangetta hollered.

Gipsy watched nervously as sixty rowdy T. rexes came piling into the room, squabbling and fighting over who sat where. Thickhead McBrick made his way through the scaly scrum and sat down close to Fangetta. He winked at her, and she winked back.

"Those two seem surprisingly friendly," murmured Gipsy.

But Teggs seemed more interested in his last supper. "This spaghetti isn't just tough, it tastes revolting!" he spluttered, coming up for air. "But I'm so hungry I could eat *anything* . . ."

Meanwhile, Braxus had battled his way over to the main doors. "Stop fighting, you lot!" he shouted at the guests. "Welcome His Royal Nastiness . . . King Groosum the Great!"

Gipsy and Iggy gulped as Braxus
led the king inside and everyone
clapped and cheered. King Groosum
was massive, taller
and scarier than
any T. rex they
had ever seen —
very nearly the
size of a house!
He wore dirty
purple robes
and a necklace
of dinosaur
skulls around
his fat, blubbery
neck. He roared in the guests' faces and
whacked them with his tail, and they
loved it.

At last the king reached his throne.
"Sorry me late," he said. "Me just taken
someone's hand in marriage." He pulled

a gory claw from under his cloak and waved it around. "BUT ME NO LIKE THE REST OF HER!"

The room shook with laughter as King Groosum swallowed the claw and burped loudly. Then Fangetta stood up and cleared her throat. "And now us would like to present His Royal Nastiness with his long-lost treasure!"

Braxus threw back the red fur covering the Crown Jewels, and everyone gasped in wonder. King Groosum gave a contented sigh as he placed the crown upon his head.

Everyone clapped once more – but Braxus called for silence. "And now, to celebrate getting back jewels, us watch stealing astrosaur scum BOIL ALIVE in our big stewpot . . ."

Teggs splashed his head out from under the salty water. "What did he say?"

Braxus pointed to one of the robot warders. "Light the fire!"

"I wish I hadn't asked!" said Teggs.

The robot clanked towards them, aiming its lasers at the firewood beneath the cauldron . . .

Chapter Six

THE TOOTH REVEALED!

"That was a rubbish last meal,"
complained Teggs as the robot warder
clanked closer. But there was a sparkle
in his eyes. "Gipsy, do I have something

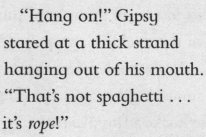

stuck between my teeth?"

"Hang on!" Gipsy
stared at a thick strand
hanging out of his mouth.
"That's not spaghetti . . .
it's *rope*!"

Iggy gasped. "You just chewed
through the ropes they tied us up with!"

"I *told* you I was hungry enough to
eat anything!" Teggs beamed. "I just

didn't want to get you excited in case I couldn't free us in time."

"But you have," said Gipsy, narrowing her eyes at the gigantic, slavering T. rexes. "Which is bad news for this lot!"

"I'm ready for some action," Iggy agreed heartily.

"And this swimming pool of theirs is a bit cramped," said Teggs. "So how about we—?"

"BREAK OUT!" they all shouted together. And before the robot could fire its lasers, all three astrosaurs sprang out of the cauldron, propelled by their tails!

Teggs landed feet first on Fangetta, squashing her into the floor. Then he whacked Braxus in the belly with his spiky tail. The T. rex staggered backwards and knocked into King Groosum – who almost swallowed his staff as he toppled off the throne!

Gipsy landed on Thickhead's table. The skinny crook tried to bite her leg, but she leaped over his head and jabbed him in the back of the neck. He was sent sprawling, knocking over nearby guests like giant skittles.

Iggy landed in the arms of the robot warder. He stuck his thumb spikes into its metal head and sent it haywire! The robot began to jerk about, and T. rexes dived for cover as it started firing laser beams all over the place.

"OK, astrosaurs," Teggs shouted. "Let's get out of here!"

Iggy and Gipsy didn't need telling

twice. They raced after their captain, dodging laser beams and slashing claws and dripping jaws. And they had almost reached the exit when a familiar figure appeared in the doorway.

"Arx!" cheered Teggs. "You're alive!"

"EVERYONE STOP WHERE THEY ARE!" Arx thundered.

He sounded so angry and powerful, the T. rexes did as they were told!

"Come on, Arx," hissed Iggy. "Don't push your luck, let's get going."

"We can't run away now," said the triceratops. "If we do, Captain Teggs and Gipsy will stay wanted criminals for ever."

"That because them ARE wanted criminals!" roared King Groosum through a mouthful of staff.

"No!" Arx shouted, waving a golden,

gleaming bundle of bits up in the air. "Because I just happen to be holding the *real* T. rex Crown Jewels! Your Majesty, those ones you've been given are FAKES!"

Teggs and Gipsy gasped. Iggy's jaw dropped. Most of the T. rexes looked confused.

But Braxus, Fangetta and Thickhead looked at each other and said: "Uh-oh!"

"A few hours ago I was digging a tunnel beneath the prison," Arx went on. "The tunnel roof caved in and I only just managed to dig myself out. I emerged in the middle of Mrs Fangetta's office, and found these treasures stuffed in her cupboard." He marched up to King Groosum and placed them in front of him. "See?"

Fangetta, looking a bit squashed, sneered at Arx. "You lie! *Them* the fakes!"

"No!" growled King Groosum, plucking half a staff from his mouth. "Me chew my staff many times. It never taste as cheap and muck-worthy as this." He grabbed Arx's staff and nibbled the end. "Yes! This REAL staff! Me recognize my toothmarks!"

Thickhead, Fangetta and Braxus all started to run – but Teggs, Iggy and Gipsy tripped them up. They fell flat on their faces and the astrosaurs sat on their backs to hold them down.

"These three greedy T. rexes tried to trick us all," Arx explained.

"But how?" asked Teggs. "What's been going on?"

"Confess, Thickhead," Gipsy warned him. "Or I'll jab you somewhere you won't like!"

"All right." Thickhead sighed. "Me really *did* steal Crown Jewels from King's palace. And me hide them good."

"But you couldn't sell them while you were stuck in prison," said Arx. "So you did a deal with Mrs Fangetta, didn't you? You said that she and her boyfriend, Braxus, could share the loot with you in exchange for your freedom!"

Thickhead nodded. "It be true."

"Oh, *I* get it now!" said Teggs angrily. "For you to go free, someone else had to be found guilty."

"And that meant framing them with a fake set of jewels," Gipsy added. "So you could go off and sell the real ones later!"

Braxus glared at Thickhead. "Whatever you do, do not tell them that unmarked spaceship was mine, or that me tipped off the Royal Rex Police about where to find it – or else!"

"Or that me made the fake jewels and done the distress call," said Fangetta quickly.

"You dino-dimwits!" Iggy yelled. "You just told us yourselves!"

"Oh no!" wailed Fangetta and Braxus. He covered her mouth and she covered his, while the other T. rexes laughed and jeered at them.

Then King Groosum
reared up to his full,
horrifying height
and looked down at
the astrosaurs. "It
look like me must thank
you for finding real Crown Jewels.
So – me will not eat you."

Teggs gave him a crooked smile.
"How generous!"

"Me let you all go free," King
Groosum declared grandly. "But these
three tricksters be staying right here in
prison for very, VERY long time."

Gipsy, Teggs and Iggy jumped up
from their fallen foes as robot warders
came to take the T. rex trio to the cells.

"Astrosaur scum!" snarled Fangetta.

"We get you for this!" Braxus roared.

"Don't think so, Judge," laughed Teggs.
"You've been well and truly *court* out!"

66

Kicking and struggling, Braxus, Fangetta and Thickhead were hauled away . . .

Teggs and Gipsy changed back into their uniforms and then joined the others in the little unmarked ship in the parking bay. Iggy wasted no time blasting off into the smoggy skies of Teerex Major.

"Yay!" Gipsy gave Teggs a hug. "We are free!"

Teggs beamed. "Thanks to Arx and Iggy."

"We make a good team," Iggy agreed.

Arx nodded happily. "Now, let's get back to the *Sauropod* where the *rest* of the team is waiting."

Teggs smiled. "Not only them," he said. "I'll bet new adventures – massive jumbo *T. rex*-sized adventures – are waiting for us too!"

And so the astrosaurs sped off through the stars to find them.

THE END